BY
Lynn Plourde

BOOK FAIR DAY

ILLUSTRATED BY
Thor Wickstrom

Dutton Children's Books

To Steph, the fairest editor
in all the land of books
—L.P.

For my sister Valerie,
who always had "her nose in a book"
Love
T.W.

DUTTON CHILDREN'S BOOKS
A division of Penguin Young Readers Group
Published by the Penguin Group • Penguin Group (USA) Inc., 375 Hudson Street,
New York, New York 10014, U.S.A. • Penguin Group (Canada), 90 Eglinton Avenue
East, Suite 700, Toronto, Ontario, Canada M4P 2Y3 (a division of Pearson
Penguin Canada Inc.) • Penguin Books Ltd, 80 Strand, London WC2R ORL,
England • Penguin Ireland, 25 St Stephen's Green, Dublin 2, Ireland (a division
of Penguin Books Ltd) • Penguin Group (Australia), 250 Camberwell Road,
Camberwell, Victoria 3124, Australia (a division of Pearson Australia Group Pty
Ltd) • Penguin Books India Pvt Ltd, 11 Community Centre, Panchsheel Park, New
Delhi – 110 017, India • Penguin Group (NZ), Cnr Airborne and Rosedale Roads,
Albany, Auckland 1310, New Zealand (a division of Pearson New Zealand Ltd) •
Penguin Books (South Africa) (Pty) Ltd, 24 Sturdee Avenue, Rosebank,
Johannesburg 2196, South Africa • Penguin Books Ltd, Registered Offices:
80 Strand, London WC2R ORL, England

Text copyright © 2006 by Lynn Plourde
Illustrations copyright © 2006 by Thor Wickstrom

CIP Data is available.

Published in the United States by Dutton Children's Books,
a division of Penguin Young Readers Group
345 Hudson Street, New York, New York 10014
www.penguin.com/youngreaders

Designed by Irene Vandervoort

Manufactured in China   First Edition

0-525-47696-2

1 3 5 7 9 10 8 6 4 2

Book Fair Day was tomorrow.
And everyone in Mrs. Shepherd's class was anxious to buy
a new book or two at the book fair, especially . . .

Dewey Booker.

Dewey LOVED books—more than he loved bubble gum, baseball cards, and bike riding. In fact, when Dewey's nose wasn't stuck in a book, he was dreaming and scheming about adding new books to his collection.

Biographies, fables, mysteries—oh my!
Fantasies, comics, histories—all mine!

Dewey rose before the sun on Book Fair Day. He needed to leave his house extra early, since he had to walk all the way to school. There wouldn't be enough room on the bus.

As Mrs. Shepherd greeted her students—"Good morning!"— she collected all of their money envelopes and put them on her desk for safekeeping until the book fair. Dewey didn't have an envelope. He'd saved every single penny he'd earned in a special book bank.

During morning circle time, Mrs. Shepherd explained, "Our class will be visiting the book fair in the library during the last half hour of the day. But to start our day, we're going to go read to our kindergarten book buddies."

"Hooray!"

"We have the best book buddies."

"I've got a great story to read to my buddy this week."

GRO-O-O-O-O-O-O-O-OAN!

"What's wrong, Dewey?" asked Mrs. Shepherd. "I thought you liked book buddy time."

"Oh, I do," said Dewey, getting down on his knees. "But please, PLEASE, **PLEASE,** can't we go to the book fair earlier in the day? If we go last, there won't be any books left. PLEEEEEEASE!"

"Sorry, Dewey, but *someone* has to go last. This year it's our turn. I'm sure there'll be plenty of good books for everyone."

Down in the kindergarten room, Dewey couldn't keep his mind on the book he was reading to his buddy. After losing his place for the fifth time, he asked, "What time is *your* class going to the book fair?"

His buddy answered, "I can't tell time, but Teacher said we're going right after book buddy time."

Dewey's eyes grew big. "Really?"

When it was time for Mrs. Shepherd's class to go back to their classroom and for the kindergartners to visit the book fair, Dewey got in line. It just wasn't exactly the *right* line.

But just as he entered the library and reached toward the new Dinosaur Detectives collection, he heard "Ahem, AHEM, **AHEM!**" behind him.

"Lose your way, Dewey?" asked Mrs. Shepherd.

"Kinda," said Dewey. "I thought maybe there'd be a book of maps here to help me find my way back."

"I'll show you the way," said Mrs. Shepherd.

"How'd you know I was here?" asked Dewey as they headed out the door.

"I have my sources," said Mrs. Shepherd.

Dewey looked back at the Dinosaur Detectives collection and whispered, "I hope you won't be extinct by the time I come back."

During recess, Dewey couldn't keep his mind on the ball. After getting bonked on the head for the tenth time, he asked his friends, "Is that the library window?"

"Think so." "Sure." "Yup," they said.

"I think a ball might have gone in there," said Dewey. "Help me up."

Dewey's friends boosted him up high enough so that he could peek in.

And there on a book fair shelf was the new *Amazing Explorers Atlas*.

But just as Dewey reached for it, he heard "Ahem, AHEM, AHEM!" beside him.

"Lost again, Dewey?" asked Mrs. Shepherd.

"Guess so," said Dewey. "But maybe that atlas would help."

"I think maybe *I* could help," said Mrs. Shepherd. "Just follow me."

"How'd you know I was here?" asked Dewey as he wriggled back out of the window.

"I have my ways," said Mrs. Shepherd, wriggling herself out.

Dewey took one last glance at *The Amazing Explorers Atlas* and whispered, "I hope you won't be lost by the time I come back."

After lunch, Mrs. Shepherd's class noticed that the door to the hamster cage was open and the cage was empty.

"Yikes, where'd Bucky go?"

"Maybe he went looking for something to eat."

"Hurry, everyone, find Bucky!"

All of Mrs. Shepherd's students skittered and scattered to find their furry friend.

Dewey crawled down the hall, looking for tiny paw prints. As Dewey passed the fifteenth door in the hallway, he realized where he was.

Dewey crawled into the library. And there, right before his nose, was the Private Eye series.

But just as Dewey reached for the books, he heard "Ahem, AHEM, **AHEM!**" above him.

"Did you think Bucky was hiding in a book, Dewey?" asked Mrs. Shepherd.

"No," answered Dewey. "But maybe if I knew how to spy, I could find him faster."

"Not necessary," said Mrs. Shepherd. "We already did."

"How'd you know I was here?" asked Dewey.
"I have my secrets," said Mrs. Shepherd.

As they left, Dewey gave one last, longing look
at the Private Eye series and whispered, "I hope you'll
still be around to investigate by the time I come back."

FINALLY, Mrs. Shepherd announced, "Class, it's time to visit the book fair."

"Yippee!"

"Let's go."

"Can't wait to see what they have this year."

"I hope there'll be a *few* books left," groaned Dewey.

Mrs. Shepherd passed the students' money back to them and told them to line up. Everyone elbowed and jostled to try to get next to Dewey.

At the book fair, before Dewey could even open a single book, his classmates begged and pestered him.

"Dewey, what do you think of these new fantasies?"

"Dewey, have you read this book—should I get it?"

"Dewey, can you help me find a book I'd like?"

"Dewey, what do you think of this author?"

"Dewey, what do you recommend for me?"

"Dewey!"

"Dewey?"

"Dewey?"

"Dewey!"

By the time Dewey had helped his twentieth classmate, Mrs. Shepherd announced, "Okay, everyone. Time to head back to our classroom and get ready to go home."

Dewey was dumbstruck. "Oh no . . . but I haven't . . . there are NO books left!" he cried as he looked at the bare book displays.

Just then he heard "Ahem, AHEM, **AHEM!**" from underneath a table. Mr. Opus, the librarian, peeked his head out and asked . . .

"Looking for these, Dewey?"

"How did you know?" exclaimed Dewey when he saw the box filled with the Dinosaur Detectives collection, *The Amazing Explorers Atlas*, and the Private Eye series.

"Let's just say we can read you like a book," said Mrs. Shepherd with a super-size smile.

Dewey had just enough money to buy
all the new books he wanted.

At the end of the day, Mrs. Shepherd hustled and bustled her students onto the bus. "Bye. See you tomorrow. Don't stay up too late reading your new books."

Dewey reminded Mrs. Shepherd that he would be walking home today instead of taking the bus. She helped him load his book buggy and waved good-bye.

Dewey hurried and scurried all the way home.

He couldn't wait to get lost in all his new books.

PRIVATE EYE AND THE CUP OF CHAI

DRAGON RIDER

WIZARD WARRIOR

DINOSAUR DETECTIVES
THE MISSING BONE

PRIVATE EYE AND THE SCARLET DYE

FRED FORGOT

Famous Explorers